FOR PURA
–T.C.

FOR MONIKA MUKHERJEE
AND MONIKA BANG CAMPBELL
–B.B.

A woodcutter and his wife
had no child.
One night the woodcutter's wife
had a dream.
Shustee, the goddess of children,
came to her and said,
"Find a cucumber.
Eat the cucumber and soon
you will have a wonderful son."
The happy wife told the woodcutter
what Shustee had said.

The next morning in the forest

the woodcutter met

a bent-over old woman.

She leaned on a stick and walked

guti-humpety, guti-humpety.

Opening her purse,

she gave the woodcutter

a tiny cucumber, saying,

"Tell your wife

to do exactly as I say.

She must wait seven days,

then must eat

the whole cucumber.

She must wait
seven days,
then eat it,
stem and all."

The woodcutter ran home
to tell his wife the news.
"Oh, wife," he said,
"see what Mother Shustee sent!
But you must not eat it yet.
You must put it on the shelf
and then wait seven days."

But he forgot to say

that she must eat

the whole thing.

He went back to the forest.

The woodcutter's wife
said to herself,
"Why must I wait
for seven whole days?"
She ate the cucumber,
and she threw the stem away.

The woodcutter came home

and saw the stem.

"Oh, wife, you did not wait!"

he said.

"And you did not eat it all!

Quickly, quickly, eat the stem!"

So the wife ate the stem.

In eighteen winks a tiny boy

was sitting in her lap.

He was two fingers tall.

He had a pigtail

four fingers long.

13

The woodcutter looked at him
and ran out of the house.
The woodcutter's wife
burst into tears.
She ran to the river
to drown herself.

Little Finger ran after her,
calling, "Mother, come back!
I am hungry!"
The woodcutter's wife
came out of the river
and fed her son.

Little Finger said,
"Now I will go
and find my father."
He skipped and he hopped,
then suddenly he stopped.
There was his father
chopping down a tree.
"Father," he said,
"come home with me now.
Mother is crying."

The woodcutter stared at him.

He took Little Finger on his lap.

"I cannot do that," he said.

"I have sold myself to the Raja

to be his woodcutter."

Little Finger went to the Raja.

"Rajamoshai," he said,

"I want to buy your woodcutter.

What must I pay for him?"

"You must pay me a cowrie.

Then you must do one thing more.

After that I will give you

the woodcutter," the Raja said.

Little Finger sat by a pond

to think how to get a cowrie.

Suddenly someone jerked his pigtail

and he fell on his back.

A croaky voice said,

"Hey, rey, little man,

who are you?"

Little Finger bounced up

as mad as he could be.

"I am who I am!" he said.

"Who are you?"

"I am a frog prince,"
the croaky voice said.
Little Finger said,
"I am a woodcutter's son.
I will chop off your croak!
I would do it right now
but I do not have an ax."

The frog prince said,

"Well, this is very odd!

We both need an ax!

I married a toad queen

against my father's wish.

He put her in a gourd,

and tied the gourd to a stick,

and has hung it in a tree.

If I give you a cowrie

so that you can buy an ax,

will you chop down the tree?"

Little Finger said, "I will,

if you pay another cowrie

when I chop down the tree."

So the bargain was made.

The frog prince sat

on a lily pad and waited.

Little Finger found a blacksmith

working at his forge.

He was three fingers high.

His beard was four fingers long.

He paid the blacksmith

a cowrie for an ax.

Little Finger went back
to the castor oil tree
where the gourd was hung.
He tried to chop down the tree,
but the bark was too thick.
The frog prince wept.

Little Finger looked up.
The gourd hung from a stick
which was tied to a branch.
He shouted, "Ho! Ro!"
and climbed up the tree
to a branch below the gourd.

He tied his pigtail to the gourd
and called, "Toad queen, come!
Here's a very fine rope!
The frog prince is waiting
with his heart full of hope."
The toad queen climbed down
Little Finger's pigtail.

The stick and the gourd came too.
Little Finger helped them all
to climb to the ground.
The frog prince
thanked Little Finger
and gave him a cowrie.

The toad queen said,
"Here's a ball
of magic spit.
Soon you will need it."

The gourd and
the stick said,
"We are coming with you.
You will need our help."

Little Finger went back

and stood before

the Raja's throne.

"Rajamoshai," he said,

"here is the cowrie.

May I now have my father?"

The Raja said,

"As soon as you have done

one thing more.

Just beyond the river is

a village of thieves.

Every single night

they steal from my people.

You must capture their king.

I will make the king marry

my half-blind daughter.
Then he will tell the thieves
to stop robbing my kingdom.
When you have done that,
I will give you
the woodcutter."

Little Finger said,
"I will chase away the king
and all of his thieves.
And then I will marry
the princess myself."
The Raja stared at Little Finger.

"How will you chase away
all of those thieves?"
Little Finger said,
"Give me the big palace cat.
Give me royal robes
and a fine golden turban,
and soon you will see."
The Raja agreed.

When it was very dark,
Little Finger dressed
in his splendid new clothes.

He took the stick and the gourd

and climbed on the back

of the royal palace cat.

Making no sound at all,

they went down the road

to the village of thieves.

As quietly as mice

they crept into the palace.

The cat ate everything

in all the palace cookpots.

Now there was nothing left to eat.

The king was very hungry.

He ordered all his thieves

to come to the palace

to catch the Raja's cat.

Little Finger held up
the gourd and the stick.
Out of the gourd
flew ten thousand bees.

The stick split itself
into ten thousand needles,
and ten thousand needles
and ten thousand bees
stung all of the thieves.

The king and the yelling,
howling, jumping, leaping thieves

ran away and

were never seen again.

Little Finger rode back to the Raja.

The Raja gave him the woodcutter.

Little Finger rubbed the eyes
of the half-blind princess
with the ball of magic spit
that the toad queen had sent.
When she opened her eyes,
they sparkled like stars.

When the Raja gave orders

for the wedding feast to start,

a bent-over old woman

came out of the forest.

She leaned on a stick

and walked

guti-humpety, guti-humpety.

She gave a cucumber

to Little Finger, saying,

"You must eat this,

stem and all."

As soon as he ate it,

he grew four cubits tall.

The Raja sent a coach
for the woodcutter's wife.
The frog prince came,
the toad queen came.
The blacksmith brought
a golden ax
for the woodcutter.

Incense burned!

Guns roared!

Drums boomed!

Flutes played!

The frog prince leaped,

the toad queen danced,

the blacksmith whirled,

and his long beard swirled.

All through the night
the wedding feast went on.
At dawn the next morning
a wonderful sound was heard
coming from the forest.
The woodcutter was trying out
his new golden ax.

kt–kt–kt–kt–kt

BETSY BANG spent more than two years in
Calcutta, where she worked on aspects of malnu-
trition. While there, she became fascinated
by rural Bengal and Bengali folklore, the source
of her popular translations *The Old Woman and
the Red Pumpkin*, *The Old Woman and the Rice
Thief*, and *Tuntuni, the Tailor Bird* (a Greenwillow
Read-alone Book), all illustrated by her
daughter, Molly Garrett Bang.

TONY CHEN came to New York from the
West Indies in 1949. An honors graduate of
The Pratt Institute, he has had several one-man
shows of his art and sculpture, and is
the illustrator of many well-known books
for children, including *Little Rystu* and
The Fisherman's Son, both by Mirra Ginsburg.
He is also the author/illustrator of *Little Koala*
and *Run, Zebra, Run*, winner of a Society of
Illustrators Award for Excellence.